Cruising Alaska's Inside Passage

Written and illustrated
by
Bernd and Susan Richter

Published by
Saddle Pal Creations, Inc., Cantwell, Alaska, USA

Dedicated to

Ingo Richter, Kinki Koi, Regina Neely,
Miki Koi and Julian Koi.

Acknowledgement:
We owe special thanks to Linda Thurston for her editing effort and suggestions.

Text and illustration copyright © 2002 by Bernd and Susan Richter
First printing, February 2003
Printed in China.
ISBN# 1-931353-09-3

Designed, produced, published and distributed in Alaska by:
Saddle Pal Creations, Inc., P.O. Box 175, Cantwell, AK 99729, USA

Other children's books by Bernd and Susan Richter available
through Saddle Pal Creations, Inc.:

* *When Grandma and Grandpa Visited Alaska They ...*
* *When Grandma Visited Alaska She ...*
* *Grandma and Grandpa Love Their RV*
* *Uncover Alaska's Wonders* (a lift-the-flap book)
* *How Alaska Got Its Flag*
* *Do Alaskans Live in Igloos?*
* *Alaska Animals - Where Do They Go at 40 Below?*
* *Come Along and Ride the Alaska Train*
* *The Twelve Days of Christmas in Alaska*
* *The Little Bear Who Didn't Want to Hibernate*
* *All Aboard the White Pass & Yukon Route Railroad*
* *Goodnight Alaska - Goodnight Little Bear* (board book)
* *Peek-A-Boo Alaska* (lift-the-flap board book)
* *How Animal Moms Love Their Babies* (board book)

www.alaskachildrensbooks.com

Dear ....

    This picture book tells you about a vacation cruise to the beautiful state of Alaska. Seeing Alaska has been a dream of mine ever since I was a child. I hope this book will inspire you to one day follow in my footsteps and visit this great state.

    Why did I want to go to Alaska? Well, for one, it has a great history full of stories of adventure and gold rushes. Second, it is very beautiful with its high, snow-covered mountains, its large forests, and its thousands of miles of picturesque coast line. And third, it is a place where one can still see bears, wolves, eagles, and whales roaming freely in the wild. This makes Alaska very different from where we live and such an interesting place to visit.

    Our cruise takes us through the Inside Passage to Alaska on a similar route adventurers and gold miners took more than 100 years ago. On the way we will visit some of their towns and we will meet some of the Alaska Native people who have lived in Alaska long before the white man arrived in this area. And, of course, we will keep a watchful eye out for spotting wildlife.

    So here's how we spent our vacation cruise traveling the Inside Passage to Alaska and some of the things we saw along the way. Enjoy!

    Love,

Here's a map just in case you aren't sure where Alaska is. You'll find Alaska at the far northwestern tip of the North American continent. It is part of the United States of America even though it is separated from the 48 "Lower States" by Canada, and from Hawaii by the Pacific Ocean. As you can see on the map, Alaska is by far the largest of the 50 U.S. states.

Our cruise will take us to the southeastern part of Alaska, which is formed by a narrow strip of coastal land and by thousands of islands. These islands serve as a protective barrier from the Pacific Ocean for ships that navigate these waters. This is why this route is known as the Inside Passage as opposed to an "outside" passage along the open ocean.

Most cruise ships that sail the Inside Passage depart from Vancouver, British Columbia, in Canada, or from Seward, Alaska, but some ships also sail from Seattle, Washington, or from San Francisco, California.

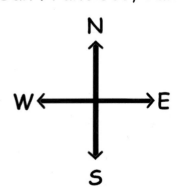

Arctic Ocean

Greenland

Alaska
(USA)

Seward

Inside Passage
of Alaska

Canada

Vancouver, BC

Hawaii
(USA)

Seattle

San
Francisco

United States of America

Atlantic
Ocean

Pacific
Ocean

Middle
America

This is the first day of our cruise. Waiting for us at the city dock is our cruise ship. It is gorgeous, isn't it? And look how BIG it is! It is 16 stories high and longer than two football fields!

How many people do you think this ship holds? One hundred, perhaps? Or possibly one thousand? Let me tell you. The captain told me that it accommodates 2,500 passengers and another 1,000 crewmembers. That's more people than in a small town! How can so many people live on a single ship? Where does everyone sleep? Where do they go to shop and eat? Where do they go to have fun?

Come on, let's get on board and find out.

Wow, the inside is beautiful! Everything sparkles and shines in the atrium, the main room that is several stories high and serves as a central meeting point for all the people on the ship. We will come here to check in with the captain, to shop, to stroll around, and to have some refreshments. I hear there's even a piano player. Can you find him?

I am glad we were given a map of the ship so we can find our way around. It's almost like a city map only it shows a cross section of all decks on the ship instead of streets and houses. The map shows that some of the decks have nothing else but bedrooms for the passengers and crewmembers. Other decks contain restaurants, snack bars, kitchens and laundry rooms. And look, there are even some that have shops, movie theaters, swimming pools, a basketball court and, of course, game rooms for children! It really is like a floating city!

Fortunately there are elevators that connect all the decks. Let's take one of them now and check on our room.

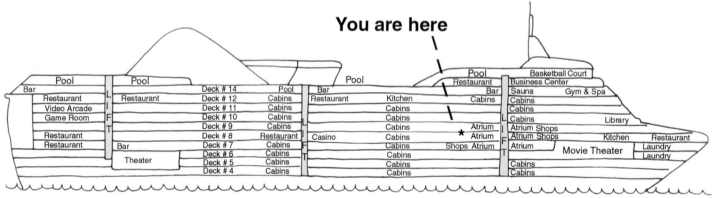

Ah, our new home away from home. Here we will sleep for the next seven nights. This cabin, as a room is usually called on a ship, is big! There are two beds, a TV, a refrigerator, a telephone, a little bathroom with shower and, look, even a balcony. With our very own balcony we won't miss any of the beautiful sights on our Alaska voyage. What do you think? Could you live in this room for a few days while traveling to exciting places?

Whoa, what is this? Are we moving? Yes, I can clearly feel it; we ARE moving! Quick, let's go up to the viewing deck and watch the city disappear.

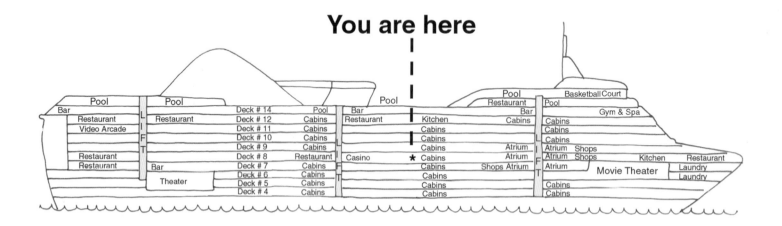

Here we are on the viewing deck and there she goes. Goodbye big city! Our Alaska cruise has officially started.

I wonder what Alaska weather will be like? They say that winters there last for up to seven months. I've seen pictures of snow in the mountains in the middle of the summer and I read that in some areas the ground is frozen all year long. They call this permafrost, which means permanently frozen. I even saw a movie once that showed people making a storm shelter out of snow and ice. They call this an igloo. Brrr, that must be cold! I hope I brought enough warm clothes.

You are here

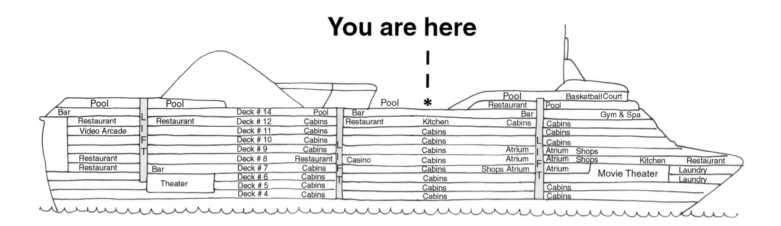

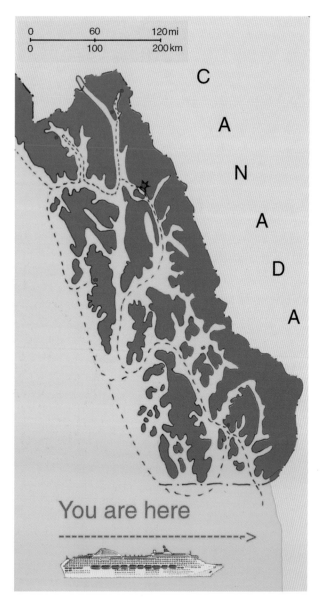

C
A
N
A
D
A

You are here

The scenery certainly changed quickly, didn't it? Instead of houses, cars, and asphalt, we now see millions of trees, an occasional fishing boat, and water - lots and lots of water. It is so much fun to watch the waves and the world go by. We are constantly on the lookout for whales and sea otters, which sometime swim right by the ship.

After sailing all day and all night we arrive at our southernmost stop in Alaska - Ketchikan. In the old days this was a busy town of fishermen, miners, and loggers. It takes a hearty soul to live and work in Ketchikan because this is not a sunny place. Some people call Ketchikan the "rain capital" of Alaska because, on average, it rains here two out of three days. That makes for a lot of rained-out baseball practices. But on a nice day like today, Ketchikan is very pretty. Just look at this historic boardwalk area that is built on wooden pilings. Have you ever seen a creek where a street should be? Can you imagine having a creek under your house? Here in Ketchikan they can. In fact, much of its business district is built on pilings over water because there is so little land between the coast and the steep mountainsides. It's just like we said earlier; everything is different up here in Alaska.

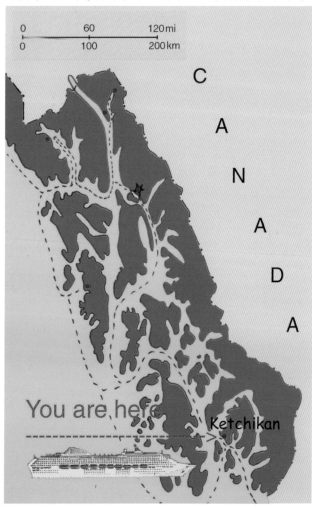

C
A
N
A
D
A

You are here

Ketchikan

Whoa, talk about different! What do we have here? These must be the famous totem poles I've read about. There are more totem poles in Ketchikan than anywhere else in the world.

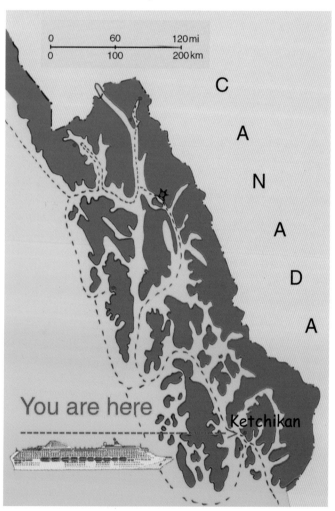

The totem poles at Totem Bight State Historical Park tell the history of Ketchikan's Tlingit Native Indian people. In the days before the Indian people had books, they carved totem poles to tell stories just like this picture book. Look at those beautiful woodcarvings. They show the symbols of things that are important to their history and that still are very dear to Alaska Native people, such as eagles, ravens, bears, whales, fish, and, of course, human faces. What stories do you think these totem poles tell?

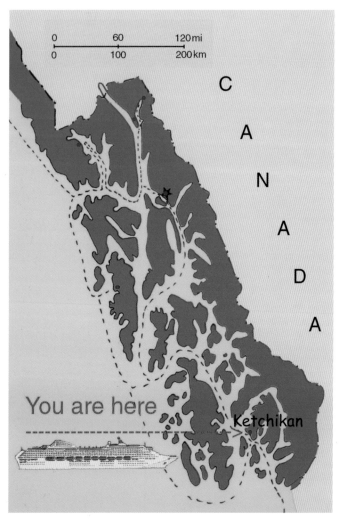

0 60 120mi
0 100 200km

C
A
N
A
D
A

You are here

Ketchikan

Some of the Alaska Natives who live in this area have come in their traditional costumes to dance for us. Just look how beautiful those robes are. Alaska Natives have lived in this part of Alaska for thousands of years before the white man arrived some 200 years ago. Nowadays, Alaska Natives live and dress like you and me. But in the old days, they certainly dressed differently, didn't they?

What an exciting day this was! Adventure makes me hungry, which is why I am now looking forward to a great dinner at one of the restaurants on board our cruise ship. Every night the chefs cook dishes from different countries in the world. Tonight is Italian night. Let's look at the menu. Would you like:

* Pappardelle al Sugo di Lepre,
* Pesce Spada alla Griglia,

What, you don't know Italian? Well, we don't either. Thank goodness the menu is also written in English.

* Homemade egg noodles simmered with tender braised rabbit and roasted red and yellow peppers in a rich demi-glace and sage sauce,
* Grilled swordfish with herb butter, broccoli and steamed potatoes,
* Shrimp flambéed in brandy with pearl rice and a fiery tomato sauce,
* Veal chop cut from the rack with sautéed mushrooms, presented with a fennel gratin and creamy homemade taglierini pasta, or
* Beef pot roast in red wine with cornmeal cakes and an array of Tuscan fresh vegetables.

That's a difficult choice, isn't it? Of course, there's also pizza and spaghetti with meatballs, if you'd like.

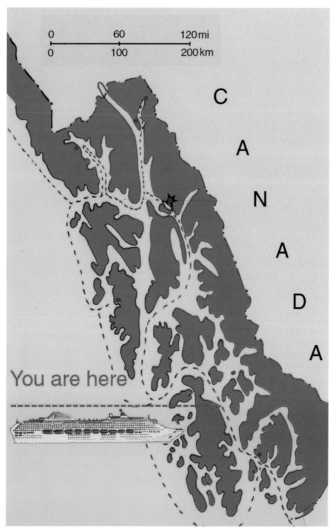

After a good night's sleep we are ready for a new day of adventure. Unfortunately, we don't have the time to stop at every village, so we are sailing past this one. Almost everybody who makes his home on the Inside Passage lives within walking distance to the water's edge. So it's no surprise that most folks here own a boat and that many families make a living by fishing. Do you like to eat fish? We tried some Alaskan salmon and halibut during our cruise and it was d e l i c i o u s! You should try some when you get the chance.

Today's port of call is Juneau, the capital of Alaska. This is the site of the first big gold rush in Alaska more than 100 years ago. Like so many villages and cities on the Inside Passage, Juneau is squeezed onto a narrow strip of land between the water and the tall mountains. These steep mountains reach all the way to the coast in many places, which is why there aren't any roads

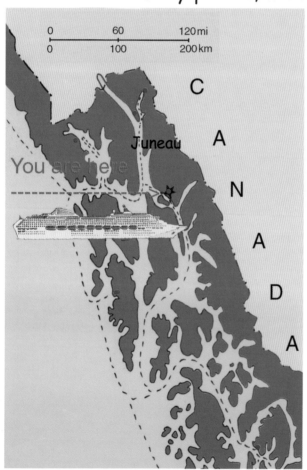

connecting most of the towns and villages that we will see on our cruise. In other words, these towns have no road connections to the rest of the world. This may not be unusual for a little fishing village, but it is very strange for a state capital. There are streets within Juneau's city limits, of course. After all, about 30,000 people live here. But if they want to go somewhere out of town, they have to do so by boat or airplane.

Look, there's a cruise ship docked at the harbor already. Lucky for us Juneau has a very large dock with enough room for several cruise ships at a time.

If you think it's strange that no roads lead to Juneau, then take a look at this! Just outside the city center is a huge **glacier**! What is a glacier you want to know? And how did it get there? Well, a glacier is a massive river of ice that formed high up in

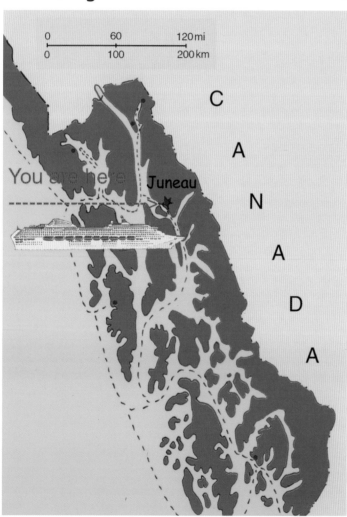

the mountains where it is too cold for all the snow to melt. When the ice got too heavy it slowly moved downhill until it ended up right here in this valley.

Most people take a bus from the ship to see this glacier. But we are adventurous and take a **helicopter**! Yeah, that way we not only can see the glacier from the air, but we can even land on it. Who'd ever think that I'd be flying in a helicopter and walking on a glacier on the same day? What a thrill! Have you ever been in a helicopter? Do you think you would like to?

What a thrilling trip that was! But there's not only adventure on land. There's also excitement on the ship for those looking for it. Every evening we listen to wildlife experts talking about interesting nature facts and about animals we may see during the cruise.

Alaska is famous for its wild animals, both on land and in the water. Sometimes animals come so close to the ship that they can be seen with the naked eye from the viewing decks or the balconies. But animal viewing is even better using a good pair of binoculars. Looks like we lucked out today! Can you point out:
- the fierce grizzly bear,
- the killer whale,
- the cute sea otters,
- the funny-looking puffins,
- and the lazy seals?

C A N A D A

You are here

0 60 120 mi
0 100 200 km

Cruise ships usually stay at ports of call for most of the day to let us sightsee. Then we sail through the night to our next destination. How do you think the captain finds his course when sailing in the dark of night? For one, he uses such modern high-tech equipment as radar, sonar, radio signals and computers. But he also uses the navigation aids sailors have used for a long, long time, that is, lighted buoys and lighthouses like the one shown here. There are lots of lighthouses along the Inside Passage because the ships must navigate through narrow island passages. Their bright light helps the captain identify landmarks on maps and warn him of rocks and shallow water that could be dangerous to the ship.

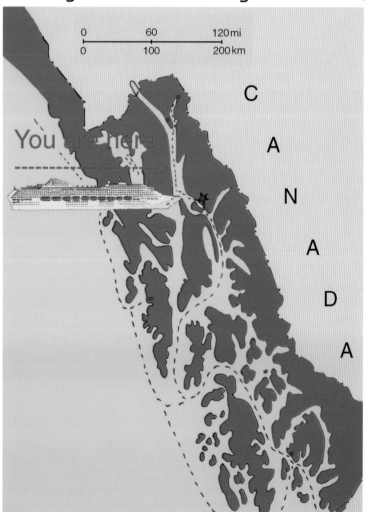

We made it safely to our next port of call -Skagway. This is the northernmost town of the Inside Passage and the only one on our cruise that is connected by road and rail to the Yukon Territory, Canada, and to the Alaska Highway.

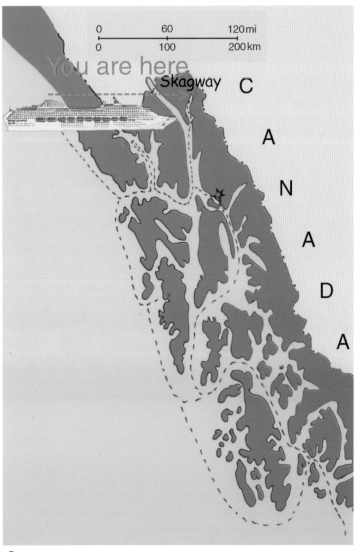

You are here

Skagway

C A N A D A

While we were asleep, the ship docked and the crew prepared breakfast for us so we could get an early start for another fun-filled day. Have you ever been on a train? There are two trains waiting for us right here at the ship's dock. So let's go for a ride! I hear the trains take the same route across the mountains that gold miners took over a hundred years ago on their way to mining claims during the Klondike Gold Rush.

Can you believe it? Within an hour the train made its way from the ocean all the way up the mountains. And what a thrill it is to go along steep mountainsides, through dark tunnels, and over old wooden bridges. It's almost like a roller coaster, only slower.

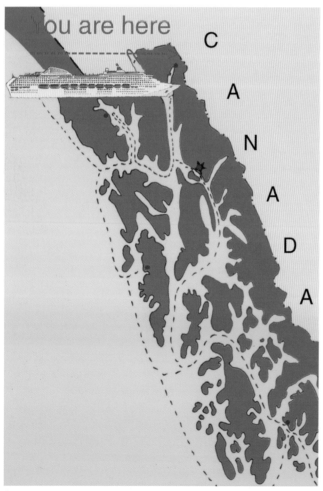

When the gold rush started in 1897 there wasn't a train here, and thousands of miners had to walk up the mountains along treacherous trails. But they didn't cover the trail just once, as they had to carry 2,000 pounds of provisions each. Even a strong person carrying 100 pounds had to make 20 roundtrips to get all the supplies up the mountain. Can you imagine how glad the miners were once the railroad was built? I read about all this when I was a child and now I am excited to see those historic sites and trails.

We made it back in time to explore the historic sights of the city before our ship sails on.

During the height of the gold rushes some 100 years ago, more than 20,000 people lived in Skagway. This is where gold miners, laborers, merchants, speculators and even some gangsters arrived on ships from Seattle and San Francisco. And this is where the gold seekers got ready for their long treks to the gold fields hundreds of miles away in Canada. The gold miners are long gone, and only about 800 people live here now year-around. But the frontier houses, the wooden boardwalks, the horse-drawn carriage, and the old-time cars still remind us of those exciting times when people came from all over the world in search of gold and adventure.

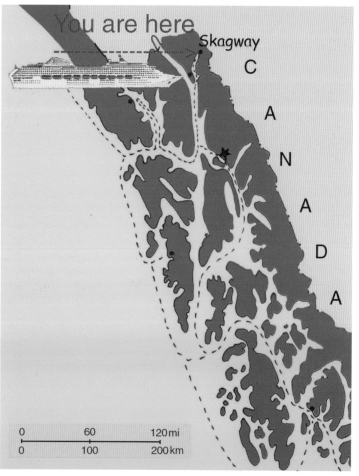

You are here

Skagway

C A N A D A

0   60   120 mi
0   100   200 km

This evening is reserved for a very special treat. We are going to the pools! But which one should we choose? Can you believe that there are eight different pools on our cruise ship? Some pools are small and shallow while others are big and deep. One pool even makes waves for swimming against the current just like in the ocean. Some pools are filled with cold water, some with warm water, and a few even with hot water. I'm going to a hot-water pool for a relaxing soak. Which pool would you prefer?

You are ......

here   **or here**   **or here**

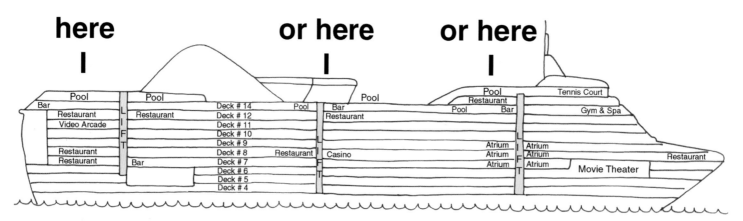

What is going on here? Why is the sky full of birds? Oh, now I see; these are bald eagles and the town in the background must

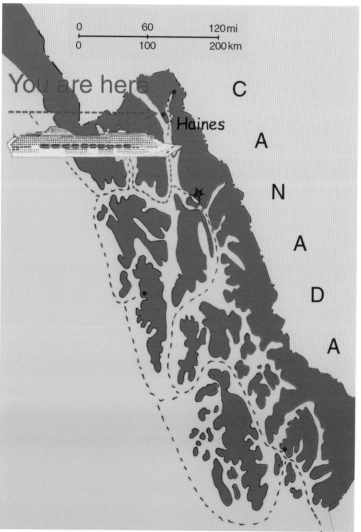

be Haines. I read about this place, which is world famous for the thousands of eagles that gather here each year to feast on salmon in the nearby river. What attracts the eagles, especially in the winter, are strong salmon runs and the fact that there are hot springs along the river that keep the water warm enough so that it doesn't freeze. This lets the eagles catch fish at a time when other rivers are frozen over. I guess even eagles like a hot meal of Alaskan salmon. I told you salmon is yummy!

Last night we cruised to another world-famous area - Glacier Bay. We've come here to see two very special things. First, this is one of the very few places in the world where glaciers have moved down all the way to the ocean. Such rare

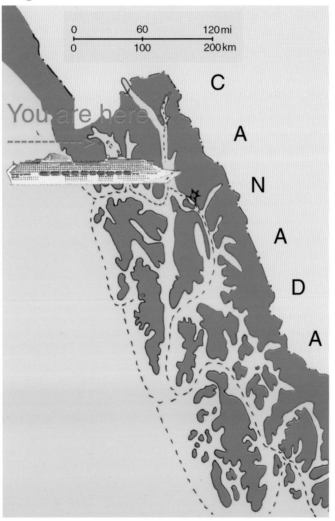

glaciers are called tidewater glaciers. What's more amazing, though, is to watch ice break off from the glacier's face. This is known as "calving." KABOOM is the sound it makes when the ice cracks, followed by a big SPLASH as it tumbles into the water. Once in the water, wind and waves then take the pieces of ice, sometimes the size of a house or even bigger, and float them away as icebergs. To me watching glaciers calve feels like watching a homerun in the World Series or a touchdown during the Super Bowl. It's simply spectacular!

What has happened now? Did our ship go off course last night and end up in Russia? Of course not! We are still in Alaska, in the city of Sitka to be exact. But two hundred years ago Alaska officially belonged to Russia and Sitka was its capital. It also served as the headquarters for the Russian-American Company, which did a booming business in trading furs. In 1867 the United States bought Alaska from Russia for $7.2 million and thus made it part of the U.S. territory. Many sites and names in Sitka still remind us of early Russian days, such as the beautiful Russian Orthodox St. Michael's Cathedral in the center of town and a wooden watchtower used by Russian soldiers.

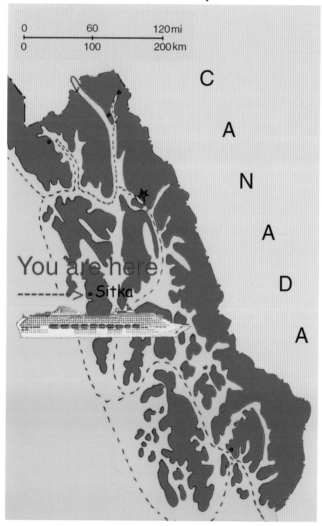

Every vacation has to end at some point and time, and so does this one. As the sun goes down on the last day of our cruise, we remember how much we have seen during the last few days and what a good time we had. We learned that some Alaskans live differently than we do. We saw some great animals that one usually only sees in a zoo and glaciers that we had known only from TV. We visited some neat historic sites of gold miners, Natives, and early Russian fur traders that we had only read about in adventure books. And we experienced all of it from the comfort of a great cruise ship. It was a fantastic trip and I am looking forward to my next cruise.

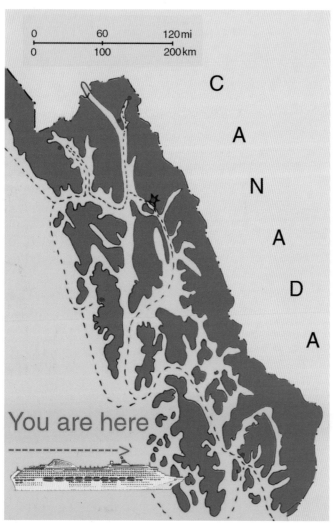

You are here

The End.

Your Travel Notes Here

_____

_____

_____

_____

_____

_____

_____

_____

_____

_____

_____

_____

_____

_____

Your Travel Photos Here

Your Travel Notes Here

_____

_____

_____

_____

_____

_____

_____

_____

_____

_____

_____

_____

_____

Your Travel Notes Here

Children's Books by Bernd and Susan Richter

Saddle Pal Creations, Inc., P.O. Box 175, Cantwell, AK 99729, USA; www.alaskachildrensbooks.com

When Grandma and Grandpa visited Alaska they...

When Grandma visited Alaska she ...

How Alaska Got Its Flag

Do Alaskans Live In Igloos?

Grandma and Grandpa Love Their RV

Uncover Alaska's Wonders (a lift-the-flap book)

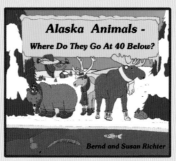

Alaska Animals - Where Do They Go at 40 Below?

Come Along and Ride the Alaska Train

The Twelve Days of Christmas in Alaska

The Little Bear Who Didn't Want to Hibernate

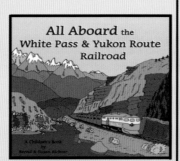

All Aboard the White Pass & Yukon Route Railroad

Board books for toddlers

Peek-A-Boo Alaska (lift-the flap)

Goodnight Alaska - Goodnight Little Bear

How Animal Moms Love Their Babies